light filters in
poems

light filters in

poems

Caroline Kaufman

illustrations by Yelena Bryksenkova

HARPER

An Imprint of HarperCollinsPublishers

Light Filters In: Poems
Copyright © 2018 by Caroline Kaufman
Illustrations © 2018 by Yelena Bryksenkova
All rights reserved. Printed in the United States of America.
No part of this book may be used or reproduced in any
manner whatsoever without written permission except in
the case of brief quotations embodied in critical articles
and reviews. For information address HarperCollins
Children's Books, a division of HarperCollins Publishers,
195 Broadway, New York, NY 10007.
www.epicreads.com
Library of Congress Control Number: 2018938080

ISBN 978-0-06-284468-2

Typography by Jenna Stempel-Lobell
20 21 22   PC/LSCH   20 19 18 17 16 15 14 13 12 11
❖
First Edition

for anyone terrified
that it won't get better.

these pages
are proof that it will.

contents

author's note   ix

the darkness falls   1

the night persists   45

the dawn breaks   105

the sun rises   161

author's note
this book was not easy to write. as a result, it
may not be easy to read, either. poetry started
out as a diary for me. so, at the beginning
of the writing process for this book, I made
a pact to myself that I would be completely
honest. that means nothing is censored out. I
talk about mental illness, self-harm, suicide,
recovery, sexual assault, abusive relationships,
violence, and other issues that may not be the
easiest to swallow. you may relate to pieces
near the beginning. you may relate to pieces
near the end. or you may not relate to any
pieces at all. whatever the case, know that it's
completely normal to be overwhelmed by some
of these topics. I know I was at first. I still am
sometimes. take care of yourself if you need
to. put down the book if you need to. reach
out to me if you need to. your safety is always
important. so, do whatever you need to do.
asking for help is not weak, I promise.

it's human.

there is nothing
more powerful

than a girl
with a pen

who is brave enough
to use it.

*the
darkness
falls*

some people have nightmares
of being naked in public,
of having every inch of skin
on display
for the world to see.

that used to be my nightmare too.

but still
here I am.

flip these pages.
take a look.

lost:
happiness.

chapped lips,
little crooked teeth,
always smiling.

last seen eating ice cream,
dancing to background music,
chocolate dripping down her chin.

if found:
please tell her
I miss her.

I don't dance
anymore.

I can point to the very first time
I felt alone in a crowd.

I was eleven.
it was summertime and
my thoughts tasted sour,
and I remember being confused
because before then
they had always been sweet.

it was like dipping my toe
into a pool of sadness,
oblivious to the fact
that I would soon be submerged.

I don't know who I am.

I'm trying to look at myself
in the bathroom mirror,
but the shower's running
and the glass is all foggy.

I've spent so much time
trying to become who I should be
that I lost myself along the way.

I cannot tell you who I loved,
or where, or when, or why;
I don't remember first encounters,
only each goodbye.
I push away a feeling passed
once I know it's gone.
it's far too painful, once at dusk,
to think back on the dawn.

I am crowded
in an empty room.

I guess it's the silence,
the emptiness,
the nothingness.
it pushes on me.
it tells me *you take up too much*

space.

I reply,
I know.

in my dreams
I feel his hands on me.
when I wake up,
I check for new bruises
shaped like his fingertips.

whenever I walk by him
I instinctively drag down my sleeves,
pull my hoodie tighter.

the body he stained
is always on display.

I scrub my skin
a little too hard
in the shower,
trying to get him off me,

trying to shed any cell on my body
he might have touched.
sometimes I scratch.
sometimes I peel.
sometimes I bleed.

this is the poem
I never wanted to write.
because writing makes it real,
concrete,
immortal.
and I don't want this memory
on paper.

I only want it erased.

I have come to the conclusion that
I am a walking paradox,
a mismatched mix of innocence and
   experience,
a bottle of oil and water
constantly being shaken.

I overthink the details.
I miss the big picture.

I am a perfectionist.
I am a procrastinator.

I have strong opinions.
I am indecisive.

I am stubborn.
I apologize too much.

it's not physically possible
to be like this.
there is a reason oil and water separate
no matter how many times
you shake them back together.

I am black and white dots
in a body shaded gray,
and I don't know which part
of myself is the truth anymore.

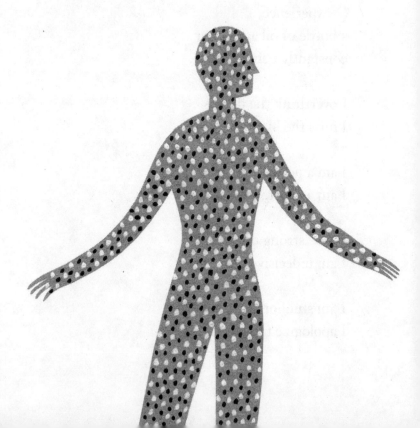

mercury:

my mood changes
too fast for my brain
to keep up with.

sometimes, I am okay.
I really am.
talking,
working,
laughing.

then suddenly,
day trades places with night
and my neurons freeze.
I stop talking.
I stop working.
I stop laughing.

all I can do
is pray the frostbite
doesn't reach my heart
before the sun rises again.

the carousel goes round and round, a lovely
place to play.
what picture-perfect innocence to fit this
autumn day.
but no one tells the children that the spinning
never slows,
that we're all tied to our horses; locked in at
our toes.

no one tells of desperate moments, dizzy and
insane,
this blissful show of ignorance no longer just a
game.
blinded by the pastel paint and chariots of
gold,
the slanted truth of childhood is all that
they've been told.

leave your brain at the door, my dear.
from here on, we are all heart and soul.

take off your shoes, watch your step,
don't touch anything too fragile.
I am brittle and easy to break:
be careful.

that way, when you leave,
you can leave without a trace.
that way, when you're gone,
I won't be
haunted by your mud tracks
and fingerprints.

I can't handle another mess to clean up.

in a world of covered ears
and mouths taped shut,
this is my cry for help.

is the sound of my fingertips
brushing the keyboard
loud enough?

can you hear me?

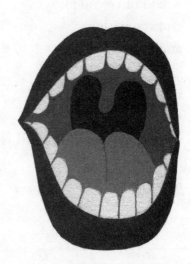

I've begun to censor your name
like a curse word.

in my phone,
your number is under
the one who broke me.
using your name
would offer you pity
and sympathy
and understanding.

using your name
would make you human
when you have only ever been
a heartless nightmare
to me.

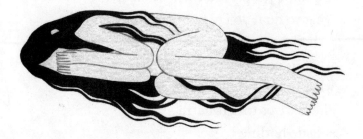

google search history:

how to cure sadness
chronic sadness
what is it called when you feel more numb than
    sad
why don't I smile anymore
how often does the average person smile
can smiling make you happy
why aren't I happy
depression symptoms
anxiety symptoms
suicide hotline
how to cure depression and anxiety
how to cure depression and anxiety without
    medication
what to do if my antidepressants don't work

what to do if therapy doesn't work
are some people sad their whole lives
what to do if you're not happy in your own
    body
what to do if you're not happy
what to do if you're triggered
alternatives to self-harm
suicide hotline
how bad does it have to be to be considered
    depression
suicide hotline
how to stop the thoughts
how to stop the sadness
how to be happy
how to be happy
how to be happy
how to be happy
how to be happy
how to be happy
how to be happy
how to be happy
how to be happy
how to be happy
how to be happy
how to be happy

I am going stir-crazy
inside my skull,
peeling off the wallpaper
with short, bitten nails.

there are no
emergency exits here:

I am left to
claw myself out.

there's blood on the bathroom floor again,
my mother would be ashamed.
my head is the one that's guilty,
but my soul is always blamed.
three months older, three months clean,
I thought that I might win.
but once again I find myself
digging graves into my skin.

no amount of promises
can make or break the fight;
do not believe that I am well
from the sonnets that I write.
it's survival of the fittest,
not everyone will thrive.
we're pushed so far that we go against
the instinct to survive.

these words are
not polished.
these words are
not pure.

these words are
venom purged from my veins
and poured out
on paper.

these words
are
poetic poison.

I cower as I walk through the hallway
like I am lost in the woods—
dodging the people,
dodging the trees,
dodging the lurking faces
behind each corner.

I am the little girl in every fable,
every folktale.
the powerless child,
the innocent face,
red hood up and basket in hand.
we all know what comes next.

I catch a glimpse of the wolf in the shadows.
the glowing eyes,
the curling lip,

the pointed teeth ready to attack—
and I realize he is wearing your clothing.

you have turned me into prey.
and you have always been the predator.

venus:

can you hear my vertebrae
cracking under the stress?

can you see my shoulders caving in
under the expectations?

can you feel my skin splitting
and the magma pouring out?

I am nearing the inevitable.
my spine will give out.
my shoulders will snap.
my skin will break down.

I can only
withstand so much.

you held my wrists, propped me up, and moved
   me on your stage;
all my life has been a script and you wrote
   every page.
you set a backdrop, painted smiles, hid what
   was within;
come one, come all, and see her now: the doll in
   human skin!

someone once asked me
what I would do
if finding happiness made me
unable to write anymore.

and the answer
is simple:

I would gladly
never pick up another pen.

where is the happy?

in elementary school,
I would burst out laughing
in the middle of class.

I was loud and outgoing,
messy
and funny
and happy.

but somewhere along the line I lost it.
the freedom.
the innocence.

sometimes I imagine my younger self
and I worry she wouldn't recognize me.

she looks up at me with pigtails.
there are gaps in her mouth
where wiggly teeth have fallen out.

where is the happy?
she says,
her big brown eyes open wide.

and I never have an answer.

I work so hard
to be the hero.

but then I sabotage myself,
picking out poisoned apples
and eating them like candy.

I am the antagonistic
protagonist
of my own story.

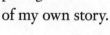

darkness awaits me; I hear it whispering my
name,
calling me back to the place I seem to belong.

most people are afraid of its voice.
not me.
this steady sadness,
this numbness that holds me sweetly like a
lover,
it runs through each artery like the life that
never was.

if this is my demise, then prepare me for
peaceful destruction.

I give and give
and give,
even when it hurts me—
even if they've hurt me—
until there's nothing left
of me at all.

sacrifice is not as glamorous
as it's made out to be.

copy
imprint those around you
onto yourself.
become a sculpture of body parts,
a myriad of unfamiliar fingers and teeth.
pick and choose who you want to be,
and stand as their mirror.

paste
take a model from a magazine
and wear her like a shield.
give yourself time for the glue to dry,
let the eyelashes stick
and the spot cream harden.
remember your skin's tape
is not double-sided.

cut
rip yourself apart when you feel
your pixelated skin is failing you.
dig back to the bottom,
desperately trying to find yourself again.
slash the imperfection away.

quit
reach the point where your screen is frozen.
you have tried too hard to wait it out.
all you are is a blank paper with
bits of plagiarized pieces
bandaging broken margins.
it only takes one press of a finger
to shut it all down.

*"what you can do
when you press control"*

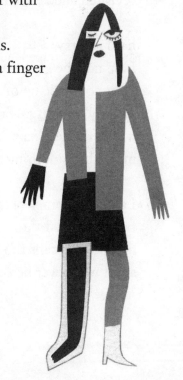

right now, I am a rough draft;
I am here to be
revisited and revised.

hard as I try,
I am not the girl poets speak of.
I am not made up of ocean tides
and my heart is not a crystal drum;
it will always be a weapon
more than anything.

I am an incomplete masterpiece,
full of crossed-out words and changes.
no one ever calls the first draft beautiful,
and I will never be the final piece.

go ahead and fight me, I'll surely let you win,
comment on my body and I'll make myself
    grow thin.
you're digging nails into all the bruises that
    you kissed,
I'm putty in your hand, but all you do is clench
    your fist.

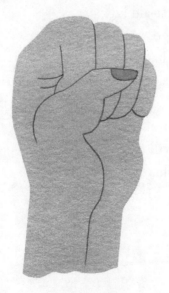

earth:

I burn and smoke
to keep others warm,
forgetting that
I need to breathe.

I carry a first-aid kit
wherever I go,
forgetting that
I need to heal.

I give out love
to all who will take it,
forgetting that
I need some for *myself.*

I am dying
in order to keep
everyone around me alive.

digging up your arteries
to find proof of something more—
I want to see blood or bone or nerves
or anything at all
therehastobesomethingmore
(right?)

a never-ending search,
a hollow hole,
a space inside a sentence.
I tried to scratch under the surface,
but you are all skin and skin and skin.

I want so badly
to spill out my soul
onto these pages,
but some things
are stuck.

some memories
cling to the sides
of my spirit
no matter how much
I try to scrape them out.

I don't remember when
my life turned into
a series of secrets
I swallow down
every time they try
to come back up,
a collection
of russian nesting dolls
taped shut so that
no one gets inside.

I have become trauma
packed inside intrusive thought
packed inside scar tissue
packed inside brain tissue
packed inside skull.

I have become
an ever-growing ring of defenses
so that no one can find
what is at my core.

for once, I wish I could be the poem
instead of the poet I've been.
rather than forming metaphors on my tongue
they'd be draped on top of my skin.

for once, I wish I could be the receiver,
instead of handing out pieces of heart.
as a writer, a lover—I seem to be destined
to give as I'm falling apart.

the
night
persists

lost:
innocence.

short hair,
big brown eyes,
almost always wears pink.

last seen in large, round goggles,
diving into ice-cold water
just to feel fearless.

if found:
please tell her
I miss her.

I am not fearless
anymore.

*"it seems like you're writing
the same thing over and over again."*

that's because I am.

I write about this—
the sadness,
the backpack of melancholy
that digs into my shoulder blades—
because each poem
isn't authentic enough.
I keep pouring out my soul,
but the emotion
gets lost in translation.

I write about this
because there is nothing

else inside me to dig up.
no more ideas. no more muses.
just dirt.
I write about this
because I need
to find myself again.
and every poem that comes out
is just another poster for a missing person—
the person I used to be,
the person I want to be,
the person I was supposed to be.

I will write about this,
over and over and over,
until I find them.

so, yes.
maybe I am writing the same thing
over and over
and over.
but I have no choice.

how else am I
supposed to find myself?

I am walking on creaky floorboards waiting
    for a crack—
waiting for something to give out underneath
    me.
I used to be reckless.
I used to jump and run and dance
(because you told me to—
but it was my fault for listening).

now, I know better.
I've learned from experience
that there are always splinters in the wood,
tacks on the ground,
a support beam missing.
the arches of my feet will collapse
and I will fall through.

one day
(it may be tomorrow,
it may be next week,
it may be next year)
you will see who
I really am,
and
(crack)
"oh no"
(crack)
"I didn't want you to get attached"
(crack)
"this isn't right"
(falling)
"I'm sorry"
(gone).

are you fine with this?
it is all I can give you;
bones instead of skin.

all is fair when love's a war,
and every day is a fight.
tongues become the sharpest of swords
as they clash over wrong and right.

aphrodite and ares are playing their game,
mixing their potions for fun.
this love is a war and the battle is here:
kiss the bullet and load the gun.

come and sit with me.
we can watch the day grow dark
as we do the same.

he told me that I could stop if I didn't like it—
but that he knew I'd like it. it's been six months
and I can still feel his hand creeping down
my side. I feel it tugging at my shirt, sliding
between layers before I push it away. he said
he knew I'd like it. it's been six months and I
still can't sit on the basement couch without
thinking of the day I said I didn't want to do
anything and he pulled my arm and led me
upstairs. he didn't want to pressure me, he said.
it was just natural, he said. he knew I'd like it,
he said. I just hadn't tried. it's been six months
and I still shy away when anyone tries to touch
me that way. because an arm over the shoulder
leads to a hand tracing down the back. he said
he knew I'd like it. it's been six months and
I no longer sleep soundly, dreaming about

zippers and sweaty palms and being too scared
to say no. I never said no. I said I guess, I said
I'm scared, I said if you want to, I said I don't
think I can do this, I said I'm sorry—or I said
nothing at all. he told me that I could stop if
I didn't like it. but that he knew I'd like it. it's
been six months and my brain still tells me I
should've liked it. I was supposed to like it. I
was supposed to like it. I was supposed to like
it. I was supposed to like it. I was supposed to
like it. I was supposed to like it. I was supposed
to like it. I was supposed to like it. I was
supposed to like it. I was supposed to like it. I
was supposed to like it. I was supposed to like
it. I was supposed to like it. I was supposed to
like it. I was supposed to like it. I was supposed
to like it. I was supposed to like it. I was
supposed to like it. I was supposed to like it. I
was supposed to like it. I was supposed to like
it. I was supposed to like it. I was supposed to
like it. I was supposed to like it. I was supposed
to like it. I was supposed to like it. I was
supposed to like it. I was supposed to like it. I
was supposed to like it. I was supposed to like
it. I was supposed to like it. I was supposed to
like it. I was supposed to like it.

three months into treatment
my therapist asks,
does anyone know about
your depression?

I perk up.
my depression?

I never thought it was
bad enough
or serious enough
or devastating enough
for a diagnosis.
I had myself convinced
I was making it up.

caroline,
she looks at me—

hunched over,
sitting on the couch—
why do you think you're here?

question:

how will
my mental illness
affect my
romantic relationships?

what will happen
when I become
emotionally vulnerable?

will they stay?

hypothesis:

if my significant other
sees all the symptoms
of my mental illness,
then they will leave.

if my significant other
sees all the symptoms
of my mental illness,
then they will decide
it is not worth it.

they will decide
I am not worth it.

materials:

one (1) emotionally
dependent teenager,
struggling with
depression and anxiety,
who believes she
is unlovable.
I have volunteered
to be this test subject.

four (4) people willing
to let me into their lives.
each one will become
an experimental group.
they should believe
they can save me,

or fix me,
or ignore me,
or at least put up with me.

unlimited (∞) triggers.
these are necessary
in order to bring out
my symptoms.

unfortunately,
there is no control
for this experiment because
I will always have the sadness.
there is no way to
extract it from me.

experiment:

wait and see
how much
they can take of me
before they leave.

observations:

the first trial
lasted nine months.
he had the
same issues I did.
we were both
emotionally dependent.
we both believed
we could save each other.
of course,
we couldn't.

the second trial
lasted less than
three months.
the breakup came

out of nowhere.
his final words
to me were
you worry too much.

the third trial
did not even last
long enough to
collect appropriate data.
he left too quickly.
inconclusive.

the fourth trial
is
pending.

conclusion:

my hypothesis was,
in some ways,
correct:

most people did not stay.
some people tried
to cure me,
and got frustrated
when they couldn't.
some people didn't
believe me,
and got scared off
when I had my
first breakdown.

some people simply
got bored.

but not all of them.

and I know
I shouldn't rely on
love from other people.

but if someone else can love me,
that means it's possible
for me to do it as well.

conclusion:

I am lovable.

all writers,
we seem to have our minds knotted.
a bed head of the brain.
and with ribbons of dark matter
braided into our thoughts,
we will never be able to
comb out all the tangles.

but still,
with pen in hand,
we brush and we brush and we brush.

my memory of you is bittersweet;
a sugarcoated bullet in my brain.
and when I try to think of the deceit,
saccharine drowns out all of the pain.
I miss the way your neck curves into jaw,
yet loathe myself for thinking that same
   thought,
for month after each month, I never saw
it was what I couldn't give that you sought.
you promised me you'd never ask for more,
as fingertips, they traveled down my spine—
is it my fault for not knowing before,
if you're the one who hid all the signs?
     you took from me 'til I was hollowed out
     yet you'll always be the one I dream about.

the first time I fell in love felt like my
first time behind the wheel of a car. it was
something so common, I had seen it in movies
and while walking down sidewalks, and I had
ridden in the backseat watching my parents
together for years. but once I was in the
driver's seat, face-to-face with another person,
nothing about it was familiar. I had to learn all
the different gears, the emergency brake, the
rearview mirror. I sped through reds I didn't
even see, stopped short at yellows, stalled at
greens. my steering was wobbly and timid,
living scared of everyone else on the road. but
eventually, I got more comfortable. no longer
hitting the curb on every right turn. realizing
when to use the brights and when to slow
down. I could turn on the radio, roll down the
windows, and switch to cruise control.

the issue with getting comfortable, though, is
you begin to see the speed limit as a guideline.
you begin to see stop signs as suggestions.
that's what love does. so I forgot to slow down
at yields. used the backup camera instead of
looking behind me. paid more attention to the
person in the passenger seat than to the road
in front of us.

and I thought I'd be prepared for the first
crash, I really did—I mean, they say it happens
to everyone eventually. the films show them
in slow motion with orchestral music in the
background, and everyone ends up okay. but
I never realized how painful airbags were
until it was my head slamming into one. and
I never imagined how the seat belt would dig
into my shoulder, trying to hold me in place
when my body wanted to break free. I never
thought of the skidding tires, the shattered
glass, the shattered hearts, the eerie silence
after everything had calmed down. nothing
prepared me for that.

and once you have that first crash, yes, you
move on—you drive again, you throw away

the love letters and meet someone new. but
you never let yourself get comfortable. I spend
an extra few seconds at every stop sign now.
my hands shake as I hold the wheel. my foot
hovers over the brake, expecting something
to go wrong. every time I pick up speed going
down a hill, all I can think of is that eerie
silence. smoke rising from the hood, heart
beating out of my chest, breath slow and shaky,
trying not to cry. I am constantly stuck in that
moment. wondering where everything went
wrong, wondering how I was too blind to see
it coming, wondering why I didn't slam on the
brake fast enough or swerve out of the way in
time. one second everything is fine, and the
next I'm just a piece of the wreckage. *the only
way to prevent a car crash is to never drive in the
first place. and I guess that's why I won't let myself
fall in love again.*

when will love become greater than lust,
or power not lead to pain?
when will torture not hold hands with trust,
or greed not be part of the game?

when will writing not grow old and rust,
or failure detach from fame?
when will we realize our creations combust
because we are the ones lighting the flame?

play movie.

two shoulders against each other,
your head on mine.
next scene.

you smile at me from across the room.
next scene.
monday after school.

our legs are intertwined,
I'm lying on your chest.
you kiss my forehead.
rewind.
play.

you kiss my forehead.

rewind.
play.

you kiss my forehead.
pause.

. . .

rewind.
play.

you kiss my forehead.
I let out a laugh and bury my face into—
next scene.

it's dark.
I'm whispering apologies into your shoulder.
I tell you I don't know if I can do this.
and then—
next scene.

it's light.
your thumb is tracing my spine.
you're laughing at how I flinch at your touch.
pause.

were you unhappy in this scene?
were you acting?
you must've been, because—
play.
two days later you were gone.

end of movie.
main menu.
scene selection:
monday after school.

I know you don't think of me anymore.
I'm sure your memories have gathered dust.
and yet I still find myself here at night.

you kiss my forehead.
pause.

. . .

rewind
play.

you kiss my forehead.
rewind.
play.

you kiss my forehead.
rewind.
play.

it's just hide-and-seek.
he slipped away, now I spend
my lifetime searching.

mars:

I am tired of the fight,
tired of combat.
all it has done
is leave red on my skin
and make my own life
feel alien to me.

I have to decide:
this is where I surrender,
or this is where I finally
make peace with myself.

I'm sure you've been offered the world,
you're deserving of each inch of land.
I bet you could sew up the valleys and
　　mountains
with just the touch of your hand.

I'm sure you've been offered the world,
but my pockets have all been worn through.
so I'll write you an ocean, I'll write you a sky,
and hope that's enough for you.

don't mistake the freefall
for floating.

I did that once.

I never saw
the pavement coming.

last night
I felt it.

happiness.

I didn't recognize the spark at first.
I had forgotten what it was like.

but then,
there it was.
a flash of light.
a second of warmth.
a glimmer of hope
when all I had for years
was darkness.

and just the idea
that this might not last forever
is motivation enough
to keep going.

somehow, you got into my brain
when you called me perfect, but
I couldn't believe it

all the beautiful things you saw
were never there; for I was filled with
sadness and pain

I was worthless.
I no longer thought
I meant something.

everyone told me I couldn't.
and one day, that was all I believed, even when
you told me I could.

I was a failure.

I couldn't believe
when you said I was special.

I told you not to.
but, you kept trying even though
I was a mess.

run away.
I can't believe you didn't
the day you first met me

(a year later, I read it backward)

the trees write in cursive roots
that you cannot decipher.
you were promised
block-letter branches.

experience never quite matches up
to the textbook,
but remember that you
are not illiterate.

life is learning to read
the messy handwriting
of the earth
when school only showed you
clear-cut letters.

fights and fears for all these years,
but maybe I'm not so insane;
my birthday cake cures past mistakes
with each blown-out candle flame.

my skin has screamed through stitches seamed,
but I woke up today; still alive.
I can hold on for longer, maybe now I'll be
    stronger
for the next three hundred sixty-five.

she was radiance
shoulder blades and beaches and orange
    headphones
carsick saturdays and card games I could never
    win,
just like her heart.
but I think I'm okay with that.

at least I played the game:
poker face on, cards down.
and that's enough.

sometimes our calves would brush
as we sat watching movies.
and that's enough.

I was awkward and she was graceful,

I was nothing
and she was absolutely everything.

but for a summer she dealt me in.
and that is enough.

the problem was not
asking him
to complete me.

the problem was
believing I was incomplete
to begin with.

you always kept yourself
a few steps ahead of me.
I spent all our time together
out of breath,
trying to catch up.

you were the first
to fall in love.
the first
to fall out.

it was as if
there was a lag
in my version of reality.
as if
you were a time zone ahead
while sitting right
next to me.

today,
I saw that you have
already moved on
to someone else.

I guess my clock
is still a few
hours behind.

some days I'm okay,
while others pull me to the ground.
I'll dig through dirt searching for
happiness I thought I'd found.
the darkness scares me more
now that I see a chance at light;
that flare of hope is pushing me
to not give up the fight.

they say that I am too young
to talk about love—
that I don't understand it.

and maybe I don't.

but neither does
anyone else.

when it comes to love,
clarity does not
come with age.
let me agonize over it
just like everyone else.

the first one,
he gave me a toy planet with a moon.
it's funny,
because it was exactly like us:
my life revolved around his,
I was stuck in orbit.
he was spinning and spinning
and spinning out of control
and yet he was all I could see,
wrapping myself around and around
even if gravity pulled me too tight.
it took me a year
to throw the cheap thing away.

the second one,
he gave me a broken piece
of a bridge he'd built.

it's funny,
because it was exactly like us:
snapped under pressure.
I traced the sanded design
with my fingertips the day he left,
seeing my femurs and vertebrae in every piece,
a broken skeleton of something
pushed far past its limits.
I still keep the piece on my bookshelf.
it reminds me of who I used to be.

the third one,
he gave me nothing.
it's funny,
because it was exactly like us:
empty and silent,
no footprints coming or going.
fading as fast as it had come.
for a minute, I convinced myself
I wasn't hollowed out.
but no matter how deep I dug,
I couldn't find myself.
there was simply nothing there.

jupiter:

the doctor rolls up my sleeves
and asks if the marks are new.
I tell her yes,
but that it was after
three months of being clean.

the therapist pulls back
my exosphere.
it's hard for me to
let someone look at
the storms.
but I let her anyway.

I'm trying,
and maybe I'm not succeeding,
but it's a start.

look at the mess we've made:
two cotton candy hearts
unraveled across the sofa.

light pink and baby blue never
quite made purple, only
melted sugar and sticky hands,
mismatched colors and
two bodies caught up in the strands.

months have gone by,
and sometimes I still find
saccharine under my fingernails.
and I hate myself for hoping
that sometimes you do too.

I never told you
how much damage you did.
my limbs were not meant
to bend in those directions.

this is me telling you
how you pulled my joints
out of their sockets.

this is me telling you
how you left me with
all my ligaments torn,
disconnected bones
floating inside skin.

this is me telling you
how you made me believe
it was for my own good.

well,
not really.

you're not reading this,
anyway.

I've always
been intrigued
by hands.

how the same mesh
of bone and blood and nail
that caresses a face
cooks a meal
holds a child
can also
form a fist
grip a neck
pull a trigger.

we all have hands.
we all have the potential
to protect

and create
and love.

we all have hands.
we all have the potential
to hurt
and steal
and kill.

we all have hands.
but what we use them for
is up to us.

find yourself
in a page.
look at
where you are.

find your past
in the pages
before.
look at all that
you have survived.

find your future
in the pages
after.
look at all that
you have ahead.

this is not
the end of the book.
you are right
at the heart of it.

keep reading.

*the
dawn
breaks*

lost:
insecurity.

shaky voice,
loose clothing,
always sucking in her stomach.

last seen the other day
for a split second in the mirror,
telling me she was right.

if found:
please tell her
I know she meant well.

but I have nothing to hide
anymore.

a pillow is not a tissue
or a shoulder
or a therapy session.
but you can
cry into it.

a journal is not a friend
or a hotline
or a therapy session.
but you can
vent into it.

poetry is not an intervention
or a prescription
or a therapy session.
but you can
heal with it.

first steps are always
more important
than they seem.

to the one who will love him next:

he's been through so much.
help him. take it slow.
smooth the splinters others have left.

I'm sure a few of mine are
still embedded in his skin.

when it comes to suicide,
we like to talk about
how the person died:
a gun to the head,
an overdose,
a rope hanging from the ceiling.

but people do not die
from a rope
hanging from the ceiling.
people die from depression.

a person dies from suicide—
from depression—
every forty seconds.

I am only one person
with one life

with one story.
but everyone has their
stack of stanzas.
some people just don't live
long enough to publish them.

while you were reading this,
someone committed suicide.

this page is for them.

fifteen things you should know about me

one.
I keep my ringer on when I sleep, just in case.

two.
I love the feeling of a hug (though I'll never
     admit it).

three.
I'm a hopeless romantic.

four.
I pick around my nails when I get nervous.
four.
you make me nervous.
four.
you're bad for my nail beds.

five.
I love figuring things out. seeing things.
   knowing things.

six.
I never understood why they called the
   romantics "hopeless."

seven.
I've wanted to be a doctor since I was a kid.
I've always been amazed by the sound of a live,
   beating heart.

eight.
words mean a lot to me.
eight.
I wish you'd use more of them.

nine.
on the first day, we introduced ourselves,
laughing and wondering how we had never met
   before.
I'm still wondering.

ten.
I want to stop picking at my fingers in case you
    try to hold my hand.
ten.
I've thought about you holding my hand.
ten.
I want you to hold my hand.
ten.
I'm scared you'll try to hold my hand.

eleven.
I'm not comfortable in my own skin.
I've been told there's far too much of it.

twelve.
you make me less hopeless.
twelve.
I don't think you want romantic.

thirteen.
this is my favorite number. always has been.
always will.

fourteen.
I'd be okay not being beautiful, as long as you
thought I was.

fifteen.
I wrote this list instead of messaging you.
fifteen.
I wrote this list instead of picking at my nail
beds.
fifteen.
they're raw anyway.

. . .

fifteen.
I don't want to stop typing. maybe it's because
I know you're reading.
fifteen.
I hope you're reading.

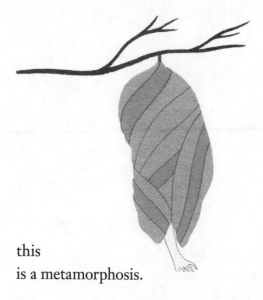

this
is a metamorphosis.

not in terms of butterflies,
where a tiny caterpillar hides away
and emerges as something beautiful.

but in terms of change.
recovery.
human development.

adolescence does not
come with a cocoon.
there is no grand transformation
to hold out for.
just growth.

ninety-nine percent
of every atom in your body
is empty space.

ninety-nine percent
of this page
is blank.

our existence
(our poetry)
(our universe)
relies
on nonexistence.

I cannot write flowing poetry
about the color of his eyes.

I cannot form haikus
about the curve of his lip.

I cannot mold verse after verse
about his skin,
or his hands,
or his words—
for the fact of the matter
is
he is not poetry.

and maybe that's okay.

maybe this time,
I can fall for a person
instead of a human-shaped stanza.

I want to be a doctor.
maybe a surgeon.

how nice it would be
to go from cutting my own skin
in order to harm,
to cutting someone else's skin
in order to heal.

love is a chemical reaction

I can't make any references to god
or the heaven I found when I met you.
I can't talk about fate or a uniting of souls.

I am a person of science,
a long-practicing atheist
with a textbook as my bible.

but something in the way
my feet feel lighter on the pavement
when I walk next to you—
how your arm brushes mine
and sends electricity through my bones
(even though I know
it's not scientifically possible)—

something in all that makes me
second-guess
my denial of something outside
of the scientifically proven.
because maybe,
just maybe,
you are proof enough.

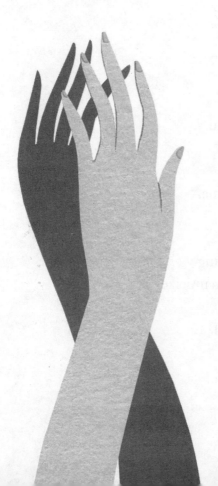

don't tell me
my brokenness
is beautiful.

this
is not beautiful.

this
nearly killed me.

this
is not something
for you to romanticize.

I am beautiful.

this
(depression)

(anxiety)
(pain)
is not.

it's okay if some things
are always out of reach.

if you could carry all the stars
in the palm of your hand,
they wouldn't be
half as breathtaking.

there is comfort
in the stillness.
in the moment between
the end of one stanza
and the start of the next.
in the freeze in a glance,
in the pause of a tongue.

the inhale,

waiting.

you don't look like
a complete thought.
you are paused at a semicolon
placed by a careless author.
I'm waiting for

the second half of the sentence
when maybe there
isn't even one at all.

but our eyes lock for
an infinitesimally small moment,
and I am calm.

I do not know
if this is the end
or the beginning
or nothing at all.

so for now
I just inhale,

and wait.

lighting a flame is exciting
and lovely and warm.

you,
you are exciting and lovely and warm—
but so fleeting.

there will never be enough
kindling for the both of us.

the happiness
will come slowly,
the way light filters in
through the window
in the early morning hours.

so slowly
you don't even notice
the night is ending,

until you wake up
and see the sunlight.

I shy away from
calling myself a poet.

emily dickinson is a poet,
I say.
john keats is a poet.

I am a person.
I am barely eighteen years old.
I think too much,
I feel too much.
I write to soothe the ache
in my heart
(or my head)
(or my lungs).

poet comes with
a pedestal of papers,

with a crown
presented by old men
in dusty libraries,
poet comes with
every word
under scrutiny.

then
I begin to picture
a young girl named emily,
sounding out words on paper
and tracing over letters,
excitement growing with
every shaky vowel and consonant.
and I picture john,
just shy of twenty,
studying to be a doctor,
but always being drawn
back to writing.

then
I remember myself.
nine years old,
writing my first stanza
about a butterfly.
I can see the piece of paper,

the eraser shavings.
I can feel each puzzle piece
shifting into place.

I remind myself that,
in the beginning,
there were no pedestals.
there were no crowns.
just emotions.
I remind myself that poets
always have been
just
people
who think too much,
who feel too much,
who soothe their aches
with the only thing that
makes sense:
words.

I have no pedestal.
I have no crown.
this—
this is the only thing
that makes sense to me.

I kissed your birthmarks—
little islands on your skin;
new, discovered lands.

I know you want to drown yourself in the
    sadness.
it's comforting to let it surround you,
heart pulsing, lungs aching
as you feel it overwhelm every inch of your
    skin
and diffuse into your cells.

but I hope you know sadness
is a revolving door.
once you're in it,
letting the sadness take you around
and around and around,
it won't stop on its own.
you'll just keep going around
and around and around.

that's why you need to
fight to stop it,
fight to stop spinning,
fight to get out.
get out of that infinite sadness.
get yourself out of that goddamn door.

revolving doors feel relentless,
but I promise there is an exit,
a surface to the sadness
you are drowning in.
there is oxygen waiting
to fill your lungs
and diffuse into your cells.

saturn:

the wounds have healed
and the scars are fading.
my skin is pale
and smooth.

I've started to confide
in my closest friends.
they embrace me.
support me.
surround me.

for the first time,
it is scarier to think
about going back
than to think
about moving forward.

our first night together,
we talked until
birds began to sing.

we were huddled together,
under the comforter,
discussing the formation
of the universe.

completely unaware
that when our fingers first touched,
it was the big bang
all over again.

completely unaware
of the infinite universe
that was just beginning
to form between us.

the closet
is more of a prism
than anything.

it's okay if you
haven't come out yet.

you are still refracting.

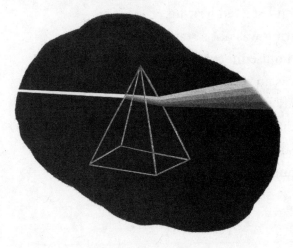

I have been called brave
for taking a saw to my rib cage
and putting my heart on display.
for putting a spotlight
on my chest cavity
and calling audiences to look.

but I was not brave
when I started writing.
writing was not a stage
or a museum exhibit—
it was an echo chamber,
a way to talk to someone,
even if that someone
was my own voice
bouncing back at me.

that was not brave.
that was survival.

but it was brave to keep writing
once people were listening.
it is hard to admit something to yourself.
it is harder to admit something
to your friends
family
teachers
future partners.

it is hard,
but I'm doing it.
and that is bravery.

september 13, 2015
my sixteenth birthday

my mom asks if
I want to get my learner's permit
and drive for the first time.
I say no
and ask her to take me
to a blood drive instead.
there are scars inches
from where the nurse
pushes the needle in,
but that's all they are now:
scars.

I am seven months
clean of self-harm,

and I am finally losing blood
for the right reason.

my veins are only opening
to help fill someone else's.

he tells me,
*you are a complicated
person to love.*

I know,
I reply.
*I struggle with it
every day.*

there are times that
I am doing so well,
I stop taking my meds.

and suddenly I feel like
the light switch
has flipped off.

and suddenly I feel like
I am not better because
of my hard work.

and suddenly I feel like
a fraud.

I try to remind myself
that the brain is an organ,

that this is a disease,
that diabetics need insulin
and no one thinks of that
as cheating.

I try to remind myself
that this is not a boost,
this is a treatment.

so I swallow my pride
along with my pills
and let myself
get better.

somewhere
there's a mess of pillows.
fresh white sheets and
the comforter pulled close,
and you—
always you.

somewhere
the clock always reads
three a.m.
the sun never comes up,
and the birds are silent.
I never have to kiss you goodbye.

somewhere
the entire universe condenses
into a bedroom on the second floor.

nothing exists beyond the white walls,
and all of space and time
is watching.

somewhere is not here.

here
the sheets fall off the bed,
the clock keeps moving,
days pass by,
the calendar pages flip.
here
I put on my shoes and
close your door—quietly—
to not wake you.

but you should know that in my dreams,
we are always somewhere.
half asleep,
skin to skin,
the world holding us gently in its palm
for just one more second on repeat,
before the light hits your window.

the mess of pillows.

the fresh white sheets.
the comforter pulled close.

and you—
always you.

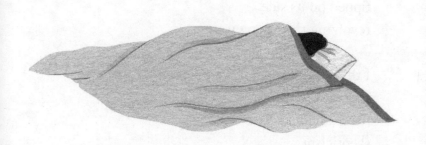

uranus:

sometimes people distance themselves
when I mention my mental illness.

they look at me
like I am a box of matches
ready to burn at any second.

they look at me
like my world is
tipped on its side,
revolving the wrong way.

I think their heads
are just tilted
from so much
skepticism.

something about us
always felt so
safe.

you could have
caressed my face
with knife in hand,
and I would have
leaned in closer,
and fallen asleep.

something about us
always felt so
comfortable.

I watched us
go up in flames.
and all I did was

warm my hands
in the glow
and smile.

but after all, the scars will fade.
your skin will heal and be remade.
the clock will hit twelve, the patches will
    mend,
summer will come back around again.
the sun will rise and minds will change,
constellations slowly rearrange.
dusty coal will turn to diamonds that shine,
for all of our wounds will be healed with time.

not all humans
are consumers.

some are predators.
they will bite
into your flesh
in order to grow taller,
and not care about
the body count in their wake.

some are decomposers.
they will wait
until you fall down
in order to feast
on what's left of you.
they do not grieve.
only rejoice.

but some,
some are producers.
they will trade you
sunlight for love
and then offer you both.
they will bloom
whenever you smile,
and smile when they
get to see you bloom.

you can either
make a graveyard
or a garden.

you can either
rot
or grow.

sometimes I think we will
always come back to each other.
not by chance,
but by choice.
there is no magnetic pull,
no right time
or right place.

the stars are not aligned for us.
so we reach our hands
up to the night sky
and rearrange them ourselves.

depression now feels
like an old sweater,
worn in and frayed
at the edges.

sometimes I am cold
and lonely,
and try to put it
back on.
but the sleeves
are too short.
it's tight around
the middle.
the material itches
in a way I don't remember.

I'm not ready
to throw it out just yet.

but
the sadness isn't as
comforting as it used to be.

I'm made of four dimensions—space and time,
  heart and soul
I am my own universe; infinite and whole
my skin is not a boundary, I'm too much to be
  contained
more than person, more than words, I cannot
  be explained

my thoughts fill up the room as they seep
  through all my pores
they'll leak out all the windows; they'll break
  down all the doors
so don't you dare define me, I am made up of
  unknowns
you cannot hold me back, I am not caged in by
  my bones

the
sun rises

lost:
depression.

tired eyes,
raw nail beds,
always in a baggy sweater.

last seen the other day
for a split second in math class,
telling me she missed me.

if found:
please tell her
she is not welcome here.

she does not control me
anymore.

you are holding
two hundred pages
of cellulose pulp
and printer ink.

you are holding
two hundred pages
of memories.
every doctor's visit
trip to the mall
phone conversation
softball game—
it's all here.

have you ever
held your life
in your own
two hands?

because I have.

you are holding
my existence
in the palm of your hand.
and I don't know
if that's freeing
or terrifying.

you can't root yourself
in the ground, hoping the world
will grow around you.

you were made to do
more than hide in the shadows
of another's leaves.

sometimes
my thoughts are so jagged
they chip my teeth
on their way out
of my mouth.

I used to
swallow sandpaper,
wear down my vocal cords,
smooth over rough edges
to make sure
I did no damage.

now, I leave my words sharp.
I attach them to
the nocking point
at my larynx

and pull back the string,
so that when they
hit the target,
they pierce.

watch as they
fly through the air.
ready.
aim.
fire.

an apology to every psychiatrist I fired along
   the way:

the first one:
I was only twelve when we met.
I spent our first sessions
refusing to speak out of spite
and our last sessions
pretending to be okay.
I told my parents you were crazy.
but it wasn't your fault,
it was mine.

the second one:
there was a basket of lollipops
on the table in your office.
I organized them by color

instead of paying attention.
I told my parents you were annoying.
but it wasn't your fault,
it was mine.

the third one:
you were the first to
prescribe me medication,
and that scared me,
because that meant
I actually had an issue.
I told my parents you were mean.
but it wasn't your fault,
it was mine.

my mom jokes that
I'm picky about psychiatrists,
but really, I just
wasn't ready to get better.
I wasn't ready to believe
I deserved to be happy.

I wasn't ready to admit
there was a problem
in the first place.

I am still learning
to let myself grow.
I am still learning
that it is not selfish to let myself become
the person I am meant to be.

neptune:

I used to think that the opposite
of darkness was sunlight,
that the opposite
of depression was happiness.

now I know that
during the day
there are clouds and rain and snow.
outside of depression
there is pain and joy and anger.

after years of flood and drought,
what a relief it is
to see the tide rise and fall
again.

to bask in blue
without being consumed by it.
to swim
without wanting to drown.

what a relief it is
to live a life
I am excited
to wake up to.

inhale.
exhale.
your body is
always working
to stay alive,
even if you're not.

fall asleep.
wake up.
the brain knows
when the sun is
supposed to rise,
when your eyes
are supposed to open.

oxidation.
reduction.

newton's third law
states that every action
has its opposite,
its equal,
its pair.

crescendo.
decrescendo.
you will rise with
the symphony and
fade out with the
audience's applause.

creation.
destruction.
there is only
so much time
before nothingness
is restored.

bask in this imbalance
for as long as you can.

this is not a journey
from sad to happy,
from bad to good,
from total darkness to white light.
there is no destination,
no ending,
no point where I cross the finish line
and collect my blue ribbon.

I'm learning to live again.
I see passion and joy and love
where there used to be nothing.

but that doesn't mean
I untie my shoes.
it just means I have
another reason to keep putting
one foot in front of the other.

I look at him out of
the corner of my eye,
past the rim of
my glasses.
my brain reminds me
that I am a silent tornado
he does not deserve
to get caught up in.

but then I remember
I am different now.
a little older.
a little more independent.
a little more secure.

this time,
I don't need someone
to save me.

this time,
I don't need proof
that I am lovable—
I know I am.

this time,
maybe I can do it right.

I spent so long
trying not to drown.
coughing up saltwater
feasting on adrenaline
kicking my legs,
even when my calves cramped
even when my feet became numb
even when I realized
no lifeboat was on its way.

I am still in the ocean.
there is still no lifeboat.
but I am not drowning.
my head is tilted back.
my legs are lifted up to the surface.
I see pink clouds in the sky.

if you think you are drowning,
just remember:

you float in water.

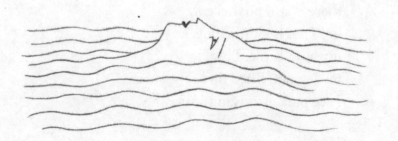

this year,
I fell in love with myself.

I told myself
thank you.
I'm sorry.
it's okay.

thank you for fighting to survive
even when I don't want to.

I'm sorry I blame you
for things you can't control.

it's okay that you're not perfect
I will love you anyway.

now,
I look at my face in the mirror
instead of my body.

you are
the most important person
in my life.

I am the sunday crossword
and here you are,
pen uncapped.

fill me in.

even if the answers are wrong,
we can worry
about that later.

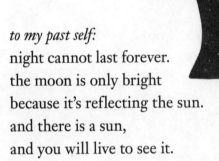

to my past self:
night cannot last forever.
the moon is only bright
because it's reflecting the sun.
and there is a sun,
and you will live to see it.

to my future self:
day cannot last forever.
I know happiness is not
a final destination
or a resting place.
that is okay.
it is more than okay.

I am not your
beautiful broken mess
to clean up.

my mental illness is not
a riddle for you
to solve,
a decoded message for you
to unscramble.

I already know the answer:

therapy.
and medication.
and pouring out my thoughts
in ink instead of blood.

you are not the answer.

I am.

be grateful that
time will heal
the wounds but
leave the scars.

how else will you
remember all that
you've survived?

the most powerful word
in the english language is
no.

it is refusal
and control
and aggression
and authority.

do you still love me?
no.
are you comfortable with this?
no.
do you want to live like this forever?
no.

I used to be scared
of saying no

being selfish
making my own decisions.

but there is strength in refusal.
there is revolution in authority.
there is freedom in control.

so,
savor your strength.
revel in your revolution.
follow your freedom.
say

no.

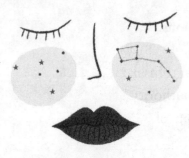

freckles on your cheek
I try to connect the dots
with calloused fingers

new constellations
little dipper lower lips
across my forehead

galaxies collide
a new night sky, star to star
twin earth signs as one.

I am done
being delicate.

as a girl,
I was taught
to be sweet,
to be dainty,
to fold into myself
until I was nothing
more than crumpled paper.

this is my unfolding.

I will use gunpowder
to set my makeup
and gasoline
as my perfume.

next time you try to
burn me at the stake,
I will burn back.

I will start a fire
you cannot control.

my professor tells the class
all poetry is about poetry.

when I was fourteen
and felt the world closing in,
I opened a journal
and picked up a pen.

my professor tells the class
all poetry is about poetry.

when I was eleven
and learning to play guitar,
I started writing songs.
it was frustrating:
I couldn't think of melodies
even when the words came so easily.

my professor tells the class
all poetry is about poetry.

when I was nine
I heard a walt whitman poem
so beautiful that I grabbed a notebook
and started structuring
mini stanzas in it.
I still have that notebook,
in my desk drawer.

my professor tells the class
all poetry is about poetry.

I think maybe he's right.

this is chalkboard love.
you're on my skin, powdered out
in sketched skeletons.

find me blank once more.
fill in the empty spaces,
time and time again.

hide the eraser.
let's lose ourselves in our hands,
residue and all.

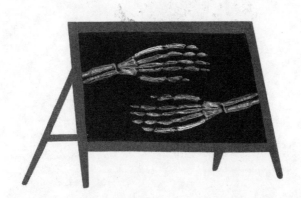

don't ask for respect;
demand it.

don't look for opportunity;
grab it.

don't add to the world;
change it.

this is the excavation
of my adolescence.

I go layer by layer,
square by square,
looking over every piece
of cracked pottery
and every stray bone.

I spent so long
burying the ruins
under dirt and sand
and anything else I could find.
trying to pretend
it never happened
in the first place.

but it did happen,
and these are the ruins
I built my life
on top of.

so now,
I dig.

write a poem.
cut it out.
tape it onto this page.

my story is not complete
without pieces from
the people who
kept it going.

a (self) love poem:

she picks at her nails
when she gets nervous,
but I know she's
trying to stop.

her eyes look
brown,
but turn to
caramel in the light.

she can stop the world
with just one
click of her pen.

it took me
eighteen whole years

to realize how
beautiful she is;
to see the light in her laugh,
the power in her poise,
the wrath in her writing.

but now
I see it.

and if she ever forgets,
I want her to come back here,
back to this page.

she needs to know I love her.

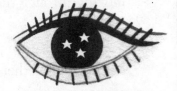

when I think of love,
I think of pluto and charon,
the dwarf planet and its moon.
she does not allow her life
to revolve around his.
instead, she takes his hand
and they orbit each other,
moving through the night sky.

both on their own paths,
but pulled together
as they tumble through the nothingness.

when I think of love,
I think of gravity working both ways.
I will not call myself the earth,
and you the sun.

I do not orbit around you,
helplessly falling and spinning
around you as the center of my universe.

that is not love.
love is when
I am pulled toward you
and you are pulled toward me.

this is me stepping into
your gravitational field.
not to orbit around you,
but with you.

some habits
I am still unlearning.

sometimes I still stop myself
before putting on a short-sleeved shirt.
and sometimes I run my fingers along my arm,
expecting to feel scabs.

but there aren't scabs anymore.

sometimes unlearning
is so much more important
than learning.

your writing saved my life,
a girl messages me.

thank you,
I type back.
it saved mine too.

we are made of
more than just
stardust
and moonlight
and poetry.

there is dirt inside of us.
there is stomach lining
and yards of small intestine,
urea and bile
and hydrochloric acid
and poetry.
so much poetry.
the ugly kind of poetry,
the kind that burns
on the way down
and hurts twice as bad

on the way back up.
it is not pretty.
it is not poetic.
but it's there,
inside all of us.

we are made of
spinal fluid
and bacteria
and cytoplasm.

and poetry.
so much poetry.

I am not pretty.
I have never been pure
or soft
or sweet.

I am beautiful.
dirt still on my shoulder
as I rise from the ground.
scars forming and healing
like galaxies over my skin.

I am beautiful
in the way I fought back
when I was buried.
I turned the dirt and mud
into soil,
and grew.

acknowledgments

to my parents for not questioning the sixteen-year-old girl who announced she was going to publish a book one night at dinner. she doesn't say it often, but she appreciates everything you've done for her over the years.

to andrea barzvi and penny moore for believing I could write a book long before I believed it myself. thank you for being patient with me, fighting for me, and generally just being the best agents anyone could ever ask for.

to sara sargent and the team at harper children's for taking a leap of faith on a random teenager from the internet and hoping for the best. I'm eternally grateful for everything you've put into this book.

to natalie farina, nicole jakymiw, and sue silver for making high school english class a safe place for me to try, fail, learn, and grow as a writer.

to my hometown disney princesses for
allowing me to be 100% myself, 100% of
the time. thank you for being the most
kindhearted and supportive group of girls I
have ever met.

to signe, alexa, catarine, sarah, ashley, jaden,
and all the other people on instagram who
have been endlessly supporting me and my
work over the last few years.

and of course, to you. thank you for reading
about my dramatic and messy teenage years.
thank you for taking these heavy and difficult
topics seriously. but most of all, thank you
for making me realize that I was never alone
throughout all of this. thank you.

Caroline Kaufman

—known as @poeticpoison on Instagram—
began writing poetry when she was thirteen
years old as a means of coping with her
depression. A year later, she started posting
it online, and what started as a personal way
to combat mental illness eventually became
an account with hundreds of thousands of
followers across social media. Caroline grew
up in Westchester, New York, and is cur-
rently a student at Harvard University. In the
future, she hopes to attend medical school
and continue growing as a writer.